Tattie's River Journey

THE DIAL PRESS · *New York*

Tattie's River Journey

by SHIRLEY ROUSSEAU MURPHY

pictures by TOMIE DE PAOLA

For Mary Huey

Dial Books for Young Readers
A Division of E. P. Dutton, Inc.
2 Park Avenue
New York, New York 10016

Library of Congress Catalog Card Number: 82-45508
Printed in the United States of America.
First Pied Piper Printing 1985
A Pied Piper Book is a registered trademark of
Dial Books for Young Readers,
a division of E. P. Dutton, Inc.,
® TM 1,163,686 and ® TM 1,054,312

TATTIE'S RIVER JOURNEY
is published in a hardcover edition by
Dial Books for Young Readers.
ISBN 0-8037-0168-3

The full-color artwork was prepared using brown-black ink over a detailed
pencil drawing. The image was underpainted with waterproof colored inks.
Opaque tempera was then applied, leaving small areas of color from the
underpainting to show through. The artwork was camera-separated
and reproduced as black, red, blue, and yellow halftone.

A young woman named Tattie lived alone by the river, and she was as beautiful as the star-flung night. She kept a garden and a cow and some chickens, and an old cat for company. She was seldom lonely except when the moon was full.

Tattie loved all kinds of weather, sunny and foggy, and most of all she loved rain. She liked to watch rain gush down the hills to her valley and flow into the river. But one day it rained too hard. The river flooded her garden and spoiled her vegetables, and that made Tattie cross.

It flooded her barn, and that made her crosser. She led the cow and the chickens into the house, where they would be dry and safe. The cat dashed in, too, and snuggled beside the stove.

Higher and higher the water came until it lapped at the wide front porch.
The cow and the chickens stared at it in surprise, and the cat with curiosity.

The rain came wilder and the river rose higher. Wind shook Tattie's house, and the waves made it tremble and rock. The water rose higher and higher. Then it picked up Tattie's house and floated it away.

Away went Tattie's house, bobbing and dipping across the flooded land. Tattie, the cow, the chickens, and the cat rode on the porch like passengers on a steamship.

They floated past treetops with birds' nests in them, past the church steeple, the school-bell tower, and past people in rowboats who waved. Pieces of furniture drifted by—along with wonders that Tattie had never imagined.

The cow stared at the rushing waters and shook her horns, and the chickens wouldn't lay eggs for three days. The cat became so interested in what was floating by that he nearly fell overboard. Tattie dipped in her toes and laughed, for it was the best journey she'd ever had. She looked down through the water at roads and wagons, and at the rooftops of the village.

The rain came harder and the sky went dark and a flock of ducks landed next to them. Tattie saw a dog swimming, frightened and cold. She got the broom and pulled him out. Then she dried him and gave him hot porridge.

The rain came even harder. It battered the windows and rocked Tattie's house so, the butter made itself in the churn.

Tattie saw a bundle of rags tied to a board that was bobbing merrily on the waves. She got her broom and pulled it in and—wonder of wonders—she found a baby, wet and shouting with hunger. Tattie dried and warmed him. She fed him with milk from the cow, then made him a bed by the stove.

The rain poured down and the house rocked madly, and the pots all swung on their hooks.

Tattie saw a plank floating. She saw a hand clinging to it. She grabbed the broom and fished it in, and found a young man, nearly drowned. She heaved him aboard—though he was heavier than she—and pushed the water out of him.

She dried his clothes and fixed him a hot meal. He was the homeliest young man Tattie had ever seen, but his eyes were bright and kind. He held the baby, petted the cat, and scratched the dog. Then he thanked the cow and the chickens for his supper, and washed all the dishes up.

The water rose so high that the treetops were dark shadows down under the waves. The wind grew stronger, and the waves came so big that Tattie feared for their lives.

Then she saw some hills rising from the water like islands. She grabbed the broom and began to paddle, hoping to make land by nightfall. And the young man paddled, too, with the mop.

On a hill they saw two fences running side by side. They paddled hard, thinking maybe they could tie the house up there. Tattie reached out with her broom, the young man reached out with his mop, and they pulled Tattie's house right between the two fences so it stood solidly wedged.

Now that they had the house safely anchored, everyone went to sleep.

When Tattie woke in the morning, the rain had stopped. The sun shone bright and the water had receded. Her little house stood high in the sun as solid as it could be.

But Tattie's house did not stand on the hill as Tattie had expected it would. Tattie's house stood—stuck fast—between the rails of a high curving bridge!

The river surged below, carrying tables and chairs and chicken coops—a wide, fast river running merrily.

Tattie looked at the young man and he looked back, and then they made some breakfast. Neither could think of any way to get Tattie's house off the bridge. After breakfast they led the cow down to graze and the chickens to peck after worms.

Tattie stood in the field staring up at her house, high on the bridge. She thought it looked snug as could be. Tattie smiled at the young man then, and he smiled back, and she knew she liked him a lot.

Above them, on the high hilltops, they could see houses untouched by the flood. The yards were crowded with valley folk who had come to the hills for safety. They were bailing out boats, wringing out clothes and hanging them to dry, and rounding up animals that had swum through the flood.

A little road ran right up to the bridge and away on the other side. When a cart came along wanting to cross, Tattie opened her front door and showed it through her parlor, then she opened her back door and showed it out again.

When the next cart came, Tattie did the same. But this time she invited the travelers to tea. They all sat in the parlor looking out at the water. It was a very fine view indeed. Tattie served seedcakes and hard-boiled eggs and marmalade sandwiches. She smiled at the young man and he winked back at her.

Tattie and her young man were married, in Tattie's parlor, in her house on the bridge, and they lived in that house for all their days.

Many a cart came, to pass through their front door and through their parlor and out through their back door again. While that was friendly, it was a bit crowded, so Tattie and her young man built more rooms upstairs, under a new roof.

Then, in the old parlor, to make their living, they served the travelers seedcakes and marmalade sandwiches. They mended their carts and patched their harnesses and shod their horses for them. It was a grand life indeed.

Though sometimes Tattie, or her young man, or the cat or the dog, or the baby would gaze down at the river and wonder if those waters would ever rise again—ever fill the world again—so they could have another ride.

The cow and the chickens never wondered. They were content to peck and graze.

The baby grew up as handsome as Tattie and as kind as her young man. And wherever he traveled, the wide world over, he always loved rivers, was always happy near rivers, as he had been in Tattie's house on the bridge.